BEN FRANKLIN'S BIG SPLASH

THE MOSTLY TRUE STORY OF HIS FIRST INVENTION

BARB ROSENSTOCK   ILLUSTRATED BY S. D. SCHINDLER

CALKINS CREEK
AN IMPRINT OF HIGHLIGHTS
Honesdale, Pennsylvania

FOR LOGAN & RILEY —BR
FOR CANDACE —SDS

LEARN FAIRLY TO SWIM; AS I WISH ALL MEN WERE TAUGHT TO DO IN THEIR YOUTH.

—Ben Franklin

Before the world knew the famous Doctor Benjamin Franklin, his neighbors knew him as Ben, the sturdy, saucy, smelly son of a soap-maker—the boy who, on sweltering summer days, snuck away from stirring soap vats and snipping candlewicks in his father's shop to head straight for the river . . .

where he *SLID OFF* his stinky shoes,
STRIPPED OFF his sweaty stockings,
SQUIRMED OUT of his sticky shirt,
SHED his steamy breeches,
and *SPLASHED IN—*

WHICH MADE BEN A STRANGE KID IN COLONIAL BOSTON.

In this seaside city of shipbuilders, almost no one got wet—even sailors never learned to swim. Most people thought swimming would make you sick.

Still, Ben swam as often as possible. He **STOOD** on his hands and shot his feet into the air.

He **SLIPPED** like an otter

and *SLOSHED* like a turtle—

SQUIRTING, SPURTING,

and *SPOUTING.*

Ben never got sick; swimming only made him stronger . . .
and significantly less smelly.

Ben spent hours soaking, asking himself **BIG** questions . . .

WILL I ALWAYS WORK AT THE SHOP? SHOULD I RUN AWAY TO SEA?

HOW CAN THE SIXTH SON OF A SOAP-MAKER FIND SUCCESS?

and SMALL ones . . .

WHY CAN'T I SWIM LIKE A FISH?

It seemed simpler to start with smaller questions.

Ben **SPECULATED** that fish were speedy swimmers because of their shape.

He **STARED** at some fish tails, then at his own tail.

He **STARED** at some fish bellies, then at his own belly.

He *STARED* at some fish noses, then at his own nose.

BEN WAS CERTAINLY NOT SHAPED LIKE A FISH.

So how could he help himself swim like one?

Suddenly, Ben *STARED* at his hands, then back at the fish,

and this time *SPRINTED AWAY* from the river.

Back at the shop, step by step he *SKETCHED* the possibilities. He *SNAPPED UP* some wood scraps and *SHAPED* squares, then circles—settling for something in between. He *SANDED* the six-inch-wide surfaces smooth. He *STRUNG ON* strings and *STRAPPED ON* straps, but skipped them both to *STAMP* some holes, until soon he finished

HIS FIRST INVENTION . . .

Ta-da! SWIM FINS.

Ben *SPRINTED* to the river,
STOOD on the bank,
STRIPPED OFF his clothes,
STUCK his thumbs in the holes,
SPREAD his arms wide,
and *SPLASHED IN—*

WHICH MADE YOUNG BEN
EVEN STRANGER THAN BEFORE.

He never kept his ideas secret, and he never cared
what people said. Most people squawk about problems;
Ben searched for solutions. He couldn't wait to see if
the fins succeeded.

He **STRUCK** forward with the paddles, **SHOVED** the water back under his shoulders, and soon **SPED** alongside the fishes . . . at least for a few seconds . . . until his wrists got sore, his arms **SHOOK**, his thumbs **SHUDDERED**, and the fish passed him by.

Ben noticed these fish sported more than one set of fins. He **STOPPED**,
        STARED at his feet,
            and **SPRINTED AWAY** from the river once more.

Ta-da! SWIM SANDALS.

Ben **SPRINTED** straight to the river,
STOOD on the bank,
STRIPPED OFF his clothes,
STRAPPED his feet into the sandals,
STUCK his thumbs back in the swim fins,
SPREAD his arms wide,
STOMPED his feet,
and **SPLASHED IN.**

The problems surprised him. The sandals slipped off his soles, his wrists still got sore, and no matter how hard he swatted and swashed, he swam slower and slower until he almost S
U
N
K.

Ben *SLOSHED* toward shore,
STOOD in the water,
SLOGGED up the bank,
SHOOK himself off,
and

SMILED—

WHICH SURELY MADE BEN THE STRANGEST KID IN ALL AMERICA.

Most kids might have felt sad, ashamed, or stupid.
Instead, this smart, stubborn, sensible son of a soap-maker
simply thought he'd made a mistake—and wouldn't stop
seeking, studying, and struggling until he *SUCCEEDED*.

And though he didn't call himself one yet,
that was the day Ben Franklin became a scientist . . .
who, soon enough, made a

BIGGER SPLASH,

SOLVING **BIG** PROBLEMS—

HIS OWN, HIS NEIGHBORS', AND OURS.

Founds Library Company of Philadelphia

Founds Union Fire Company

JOIN, or DIE.

Creates America's first political cartoon

Invents lightning rod

Signs Declaration of Independence

Creates design later used on first U.S. coin

Invents glass armonica

Invents bifocals

Signs U.S. Constitution

Founds Academy of Philadelphia,
later the University of Pennsylvania

Charts Gulf Stream

Invents library chair with ladder

AS WE ENJOY GREAT ADVANTAGES FROM THE INVENTIONS OF OTHERS, WE SHOULD BE GLAD OF AN OPPORTUNITY TO SERVE OTHERS BY ANY INVENTION OF OURS.

—Ben Franklin

AUTHOR'S NOTE

Ben Franklin taught himself to swim when he was quite young. Around age eleven, he made the first pair of swim fins and tried them out in Boston's Charles River. Franklin wasn't aware that Leonardo da Vinci and Giovanni Borelli drew designs for swim fins hundreds of years before, but no one knows if their designs were built. It seems Ben's swim fins were the first tested in a body of water.

Here is Franklin's description from a letter to a fellow scientist in 1773, written more than fifty years after his first invention:

When I was a boy, I made two oval palettes, each about ten inches long, and six broad, with a hole for the thumb, in order to retain it fast in the palm of my hand. They much resembled a painter's palettes. In swimming I pushed the edges of these forward, and I struck the water with their flat surfaces as I drew them back. I remember I swam faster by means of these pallets, but they fatigued my wrists. I also fitted to the soles of my feet a kind of sandals; but I was not satisfied with them, because I observed that the stroke is partly given by the inside of the feet and the ankles, and not entirely with the soles of the feet.

Notice Ben's letter says he "was not satisfied," not that he failed. The letter then tells of a new invention he'd seen: a swim shirt made of two pieces of cork covered in canvas. Franklin also invented a kind of "swim sail" by flying a kite while lying on his back floating in a pond and letting the kite take him to the other side. From his first invention to his last, Ben never gave up when a subject interested him.

Franklin never wrote about exactly how the fins were made or how long it took. I imagined him following the basic scientific method: Problem. Research. Hypothesis. Test. Analyze. Conclude. Repeat. There's no way of knowing if he stared at fish, or his own tail, but Ben had a great sense of humor, so I imagined he did both.

Franklin became a great success—a writer, publisher, scientist, statesman, politician, and an inventor—the most famous American of his time. Reading the list of his accomplishments can make someone dizzy. How did he think it all? Read it all? Write it all? Organize it all? Build it all? Solve it all?

Maybe he accomplished so much through swimming, an exercise that works the body while relaxing the mind. Franklin swam throughout his life, calling it a "delightful and wholesome" exercise, "one of the most healthy and agreeable in the world." I wonder, despite the great honors he received throughout his long, famous life, if Ben would have been most proud of a distinction earned 178 years after his death—he was inducted into the International Swimming Hall of Fame.

—BR

HIDE NOT YOUR TALENTS, THEY FOR USE WERE MADE.
WHAT'S A SUN-DIAL IN THE SHADE!
—**Poor Richard Improved,** *1750*

TIMELINE OF BENJAMIN FRANKLIN'S LIFE

1706 Born January 17 to Josiah and Abiah Franklin in the seaport city of Boston.

1717 Invents swim fins and tests them in the Charles River.

1718 Apprentices to brother James in printing shop after only two years of formal schooling.

1723 Runs away from Boston. Finds printing work in Philadelphia.

1728 Opens printing office.

1729 Publishes the *Pennsylvania Gazette.* Son William born (mother unknown).

1730 Marries Deborah (Read) Rogers.

1731 Founds America's first public library.

1732 Publishes first edition of *Poor Richard's Almanack.* Son Francis (called Franky) born.

1736 Founds the Union Fire Company to fight fires. Francis dies.

1737 Becomes postmaster of Philadelphia.

1742 Invents fireplace stove that provides more heat and less smoke.

1743 Founds the American Philosophical Society. Daughter, Sarah (called Sally), born.

1747 Organizes volunteer militia. First writes about electrical experiments.

1748 Retires from printing as a wealthy man.

1749 Founds the Academy of Philadelphia (now the University of Pennsylvania).

1750 Invents the lightning rod.

1751 Raises funds for first hospital in Pennsylvania. Organizes first American fire-insurance company. His book on electricity published in London. Elected to Pennsylvania Assembly.

1752 Experiments with a kite and electricity. Invents flexible catheter to help ease the pain of kidney stones.

1753 Cuts mail delivery time in half as deputy postmaster general of the British colonies. Awarded master of arts degrees by Harvard (its first honorary degree) and Yale.

1754 Designs and possibly draws America's first political cartoon.

French and Indian War erupts over land disputes in Ohio.

1756 Improves street lighting, street sweeping, and paving in Philadelphia.

French and Indian War spreads in Europe as the Seven Years' War.

England declares war on France.

1757 Travels to England to represent Pennsylvania colonists in disputes with the Penn family.

1758 Invents an improved chimney damper and experiments with refrigeration.

1759 Awarded honorary degree from University of St. Andrews; called Doctor Franklin.

1761 Invents a musical instrument, the glass armonica.

1763 Invents an odometer to help measure postal routes.

French and Indian War ends with British victory. France gives up territory east of the Mississippi River.

1764 Campaigns for Pennsylvania Assembly; loses the election. Lives in England for ten years.

1768 Invents phonetic alphabet. Prints maps that chart the Gulf Stream.

1770 **Boston Massacre.**

1772 Writes against slavery. (Franklin owned several slaves early in his life and published advertisements for slave sales in his newspapers. By 1781, he's no longer a slaveholder.)

1773 **Boston Tea Party.**

1774 Removed as postmaster by British government. Wife Deborah dies.

First Continental Congress meets.

1775 Returns to Philadelphia. Elected delegate to the Second Continental Congress. As first postmaster of the united colonies, organizes postal system. **Revolutionary War begins.**

1776 Signs the Declaration of Independence he helped draft. **The Declaration is adopted on July 4.** Designs first United States coin. Sails to France as American commissioner to establish an alliance with the country.

1778 Negotiates Treaty of Alliance with France.

1783 Signs Treaty of Paris with Great Britain. **Revolutionary War ends.**

1784 Invents bifocals.

1786 Invents pole for taking books from high shelves and a combined library chair and ladder.

1787 Serves as delegate from Pennsylvania at the Constitutional Convention and signs the Constitution of the United States. Elected president of an abolitionist society.

1788 **The Constitution is ratified.**

1789 Composes and submits first petition against slavery to appear before the U.S. Congress.

George Washington inaugurated as first president of the United States.

1790 Ben Franklin dies of pleurisy and lung infection at home in Philadelphia, April 17.

SOURCES*

The Ben Franklin Tercentenary. Franklin & Marshall
College. benfranklin300.org.

Chaplin, Joyce E. *The First Scientific American:
Benjamin Franklin and the Pursuit of Genius.*
New York: Basic Books, 2006.

Franklin, Benjamin. *The Autobiography of Benjamin
Franklin.* New York: Simon and Schuster, 2004.

——————. *The Ingenious Dr. Franklin: Selected
Scientific Letters of Benjamin Franklin.* Edited by
Nathan G. Goodman. Philadelphia: University of
Pennsylvania Press, 1931.

——————. The Papers of Benjamin Franklin.
The American Philosophical Society and Yale
University. Digital edition by the Packard
Humanities Institute. franklinpapers.org.

——————. *Selections: Autobiography, Poor
Richard, and Later Writings.* New York: Library of
America, 1997.

Gill, Harold B., Jr. "Colonial Americans in the Swim."
Colonial Williamsburg Journal, Winter 2001–02.
history.org/foundation/journal/winter01-02/
swim.cfm.

International Swimming Hall of Fame. "Ben Franklin,
USA, 1968 Honor Contributor." ishof.org/
Honorees/68/68bfranklin.html.

Isaacson, Walter. *Benjamin Franklin: An American Life.*
New York: Simon and Schuster, 2003.

Isserman, Maurice. "Ben Franklin and the Gulf
Stream." Study of Place. studyofplace.info/
ActivityContent/Materials/OceanCurrents_
Reading_BenFranklinGulfStream.pdf.

Sherr, Lynn. *Swim: Why We Love the Water.* New York:
PublicAffairs, 2012.

Talbott, Page, ed. *Benjamin Franklin: In Search of a
Better World.* New Haven: Yale University Press,
2005.

Thévenot, Melchisédec. *The Art of Swimming.* 3rd ed.
Translated from the French. London: John Lever,
1789.

US History.org. Independence Hall Association in
Philadelphia. ushistory.org/franklin.

Wolff, Daniel. *How Lincoln Learned to Read: Twelve
Great Americans and the Educations That Made
Them.* New York: Bloomsbury USA, 2009.

*Websites active at time of publication

SOURCE NOTES

The source of each quotation in this book is found
online at franklinpapers.org. The citation indicates the
first words of the quotation, its document source, and
date if available.

Back cover: "Let the experiment . . .": letter to John
Lining, March 18, 1755.

Page 3: "Learn fairly to . . .": letter to Oliver Neave,
undated (before 1769).

Page 28: "As we enjoy . . .": *Autobiography,* part 13.

Page 28: "When I was a . . .": letter to Jacques
Barbeu-Dubourg, March (?), 1773.

Page 29: "was not satisfied": Ibid.

Page 29: "delightful and wholesome": letter to Oliver
Neave, undated (before 1769).

Page 29: "one of the most . . .": letter to Jacques
Barbeu-Dubourg, March (?), 1773.

Page 30: "Hide not your . . .": *Poor Richard Improved,* 1750.

ACKNOWLEDGMENTS

Thanks to Roy Goodman of the American Philosophical
Society and Melissa Clemmer of Remer and Talbott for
their expertise and suggestions concerning text and art.
—BR

Calkins Creek
An Imprint of Highlights
815 Church Street
Honesdale, Pennsylvania 18431
Printed in Malaysia

ISBN: 978-1-62091-446-5

Library of Congress Control Number: 2014931339

First edition

10 9 8 7 6 5 4 3 2 1

Designed by Barbara Grzeslo / Production by Margaret
Mosomillo / Titles set in Ursus Regular, Mader Regular / Text
set in Cambria and Mader Italic / The illustrations are done
in ink and watercolor.